Location: Stockport, UK. Jennifer Wilson's

Jen Wilson is looking at her answer phone, her emails, her twitter feed, her Instagram. She says to herself *"She's going to find me, I know she will"*. Jen is paranoid that a woman she has never met called Olivia Hargreaves is trying to track her down. Jen has met Olivia of course… many times. That sounds like the most blatant contradiction ever made… but the explanation is that Jen is experiencing past life memories. These memories become clearer as she gets into her 20s and especially 30s. She is now 32 and the memories are now at a level as if they all happened last week. They are memories of intimate, very close and other times very traumatic events involving Olivia. In previous lifetimes she has been desperate to discover Olivia. In this lifetime she wants to avoid her at all costs due to the memories of tragedy and trauma concerning Olivia. As far as Jen is concerned her life (and indeed Olivia's life) could depend on avoiding one another. It cannot be a coincidence that in life after life everything keeps going wrong to a tragic and indeed, fatal extent.

Jen is right. Olivia is trying to track her down. Olivia knows more-or-less where Jen will be living… and therefore has gone as far as emigrating from Brooklyn to Manchester. You may wonder why Olivia doesn't just check Jen's social media? Well, as soon as Jen recalled past lives and the tragedy (suicides, cliff falls, plane crashes, etc) she largely avoided using her real name on her accounts. While in terms of phone books and so on, well there's a lot of Wilson's in Stockport and Manchester. But, if we look at this from Olivia's perspective… she thinks that Jen will inevitably try and find her. So Olivia is very optimistic of ultimate success. And while Jen is not trying to find Olivia, she is curious about whether or not Olivia is trying to find her. It is a curiosity that she cannot shake off. And this means she wants to find Olivia without Olivia finding her. Thus Jen intends to contact Olivia using her fake named twitter account so that Olivia is unaware that the person who has contacted her is in-fact Jen.

Jen's twitter account address is @MelissaUK2

Using that account she finds Olivia's accounts with ease as all she had to do was run searches for *Olivia Hargreaves, Jen Preston, Sarah Aston, Lara Hine…* a combination or a few of those name propped up together precisely because Olivia is aware that is one easy way for Jen to find her.

Anyway she observes that Olivia has commented on Man Utd's manager being under pressure. So Jen (posing as Melissa) says

"You are Man Utd fan or someone who likes bashing them a bit?"

"Stockers actually"

"You mean Stockport?"

"Yeah. I'm more into music than soccer though, especially Oasis."

Jen of course is aware that Olivia is American but pretends to be unaware so asks the question

"hhmmm… you said soccer. Are you that most rare breed of an American Stockport County fan

"Yeah, sort of."

"What do you mean by 'sort of'?"

"I am not American or British really or Stockport County really. I am a Manc in love with a Manc!"

"Oh please explain how this is or came to be… I'm all ears."

"No way. You would never believe me!"

Jen clicks off the direct messaging page. She does not want to come across as excessively interested. But she has said enough for Olivia to click on Melissa's (Jen's) twitter home page. It was Jen referring to her as American just because she said *soccer* that has made Olivia slightly suspicious. And on Melissa's twitter page Olivia eyes a link to Melissa's Instagram page. So she clicks on the link, and there Jen has made an obvious mistake. She has called herself Melissa Wilson on her Instagram page. In previous lives she had been Jennifer Preston by the time she reached 30 due to marrying Mark Preston… so Wilson was a weaker memory. The name Preston was and is the stronger memory. But still, it's enough to raise hopes to very high levels in Olivia's mind as Olivia's memories of past lives extend to awareness of Jen's sir-name being Wilson before marrying Mark. Seeing the name Wilson is enough for her to shout "GOTCHA!" out-loud when landing on the Instagram page. Straight away she emails her Brooklyn friends Sarah Aston and Lara Hine to inform them that she thinks she has found Jen. And later that same day Olivia adds one more message to the twitter correspondence with so-called Melissa. Olivia goes to the Direct Messaging page again and adds

"Nice chatting with you earlier **Jen**. Hopefully chat later!"

Jen responds to this by closing her twitter account, facebook account and Instagram account. She fears repeating past life mistakes so much. She loves Olivia but that is all the more reason to avoid her, so as to ensure that Olivia is safe. She does not want trauma in her own or Olivia's life. But unfortunately for Jen, Olivia had several hours to research Jen's instagram page before Jen shut it down. And she saw a photograph of the lecture hall that Jen had posted… Jen had commented on the picture. Her comment is…

I'm too old to be a student and too immature to be called mature. But anyways, this is the lecture hall where I am studying Psychology as a so-called mature student!

Olivia also discovered a picture of a cafe/bar called *'Delicious'* with Jen's flattering accompanying comment of

It's true to its name.

Olivia searched online for this cafe/bar, focusing of course on Stockport… and she discovered it.

Manchester has two very large Universities… the University of Manchester and Manchester Metropolitan University. Olivia regarded it as a toss of a coin concerning which Uni Jen would be attending. She luckily makes the right guess… the University of Manchester.

"Hassle hassle hassle" Olivia said to herself… as she arranged a careers advice appointment for herself at the Uni. She is rightly aware that these days people who are not working or studying at a major University cannot just gain access. You require a swipe card. Hence Olivia's plan is to gain entry and then not turn up for the appointment. But she uttered the words *hassle hassle hassle* to herself because the Uni is huge so she thinks that it will only allow her access to one specific part of the Uni.

She turns up at the building where there is a lecture hall that she has discovered is used for Psych lectures. The Psychology tutors are based in this building. She entered by pretending to be at the right place for her careers advice appointment. She might as well have not bothered arranging an appointment at all. When she was informed she is in the wrong building, she said that she wants to see a Professor Andrew Gallagher about potentially studying Psychology here.

"I have messaged him and he said if I can catch him in his office in-between his seminars and lectures then that is fine with him."

"Ok you can try him on this number."

Olivia pretends to try and get through to him, but really she wants to get to the lecture hall. As soon as the receptionist is out of sight, Olivia heads off to try and find the lecture hall. Every student she passes, she asks

"Do you know Jen Wilson? She's a Psychology student here."

After about 25 students answering negatively she finally finds one that says "Yes."

To Olivia's delight she is informed that Jen should be at a lecture right here in just a-little over 2 hours time.

So Olivia hangs around excitedly remembering the happiest of memories from former lives as she waits and ponders why Jen has been so determined to avoid her. When she spots Jen arrive, Olivia tries to hide rather than simply announcing she is here. Afterall, Jen doesn't want to make contact with her and as a result, Olivia is hesitant. Olivia's musings on why Jen has been reluctant to meet up have been reduced to two large probabilities.

(1) Jen's distrust of her own past life memories

(2) the correct reason of so much suffering/trauma in previous lives.

Olivia enters the Psychology lecture room sitting a couple of rows behind Jen. She wonders why Jen has taken so long to become a student and also why someone who has knowledge of past life memories wants to study psychology given the level of sceptism about non-local consciousness, Void experiences, Reincarnation and so on in the field of academic Psychology.

The lecturer is Professor Stephen Gallagher. He is also a big selling author concerning books on Post Freudian and Post Jungian Psychology, successful in and beyond the UK. Olivia has zero incentive to invest her focus in what Gallagher is saying and predictably spends her time obsessing about the mature student two rows in-front of her. The level of knowledge she has garnered about the nature of reality really turns the mute button on intellectuals. And this is a big confusion for Olivia concerning Jen. If everyone was aware of half as much as we (Olivia and Jen) are aware of about the nature of reality then there would surely be mass cure of a multitude of minor mental health issues. But then, Olivia thinks, Jen and her have suffered in previous lives. But for Olivia there is nothing ultimately to worry about given consciousness continues post-bodily death. Jen's avoidance of Olivia makes Olivia wonder if Jen has a different perspective on all of this… and narrow psychology still has an important role in Jen's mind?

Gallagher asks his students if any of them has a view on the relevance of Freud's and Jung's views in the contemporary world? Olivia cannot resist answering for two reasons… one she thinks it fun given she is not even taking this course that she is the one answering and secondly, she thinks its a way to communicate to Jen that she has found her. So Olivia responds…

"Surely its all about neuroscience discovering the area's in the brain concerning repression, complexes, defence mechanisms, archetypes. Maybe there's something in Jungian collective archetypes being collective that might ultimately win neurosciences approval."

Jen's heart misses a beat as she almost instantly picks up on the American accent. Olivia's voice sounds exactly like what Jen hears in her dreams. She isn't certain that this is Olivia. It could be someone else from the New York area. But she thinks its Olivia. So she packs her bag, stands up, makes her way past the other students and heads for the exit. Olivia, seeing Jen heading out, and with nothing to pack, follows her out.

"Anyone else finding my lecture so boring they want to leave after just 7 minutes?" asks Gallagher half jokingly. One comedian takes to his feet only to sit back down again.

Jen is moving down the corridor fast. Olivia is hesitant to make this a test of who is physically fastest so opts for a half-hearted effort to keep up and a maximum effort at verbal persuasion.

"JEN! JEN! JEN!!!"

Olivia changes her mind about not making this a chase and starts running… she would have let Jen get away if she didn't start to make a move. So there's one 32 year old mature student chasing another 32 year old mature student down the University corridors. Realising that Olivia is actually trying to catch her up results in Jen running into a random lecture hall at high speed. Its a theoretical physics lecture.

"You are late" declares the lecturer.. "but I can see you were rushing to make up for lost time."

Then in runs Olivia.

The lecturer notices the second student dash in but decides to get back to his lecture. Jen and Olivia take their seats, Olivia sitting right next to Jen. Olivia, clearly over-coming her initial hesitancy, strokes Jens hair and whispers into her ear

"I love you."

Jen can hardly ignore this but outwardly that is exactly what she does.

The lecturer is discussing Quantum entanglement. The lecturer starts encouraging the students to interrupt him if they can contribute anything of value about this issue. Olivia, feeling high as a kite, chips in

"Well, I have just been in a psychology lecture. But it was boring so came here… but in psychology Jung and Pauli got together and came up with the theory of Synchronicity. I think Quantum Entanglement is something like that."

Professor Gallagher responds

"Can you discuss it as Wolfgang Pauli would if he was talking to a physics colleague like Neils Bohr?"

"Err no. And bye."

Olivia suddenly feeling uncomfortable gets up and heads for the exit where she plans to ambush Jen at the end of the lecture."

Jen sits there thinking *WTF?*

At the end of the lecture Jen simply runs past Olivia who is reluctant to use physical force to ensure a capture of her cosmic lover. It wouldn't exactly look right.

"JEN! JEN! STOP! Referencing an old film Olivia shouts "I FEEL LIKE TOM HANKS IN *CATCH ME IF YOU CAN*!!!"

Jen stops running, realising that she has been totally discovered and running will not help the situation. Olivia panting with exhaustion walks up to Jen and says

"You are paranoid for avoiding me given that you know fine well that consciousness is indestructible. There is no death. Trust the process Jen."

Jen still remains silent but she now understands that Olivia has guessed right about the reason for her avoidance.

Olivia, eyes tearing up because this moment for her is the Holy Grail. She sings in a whisper into Jen's ear

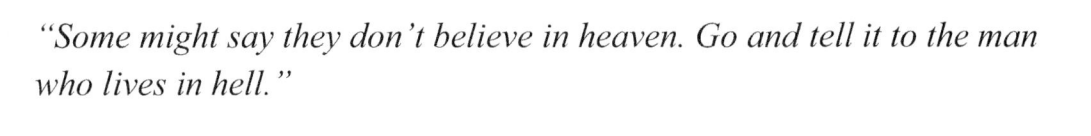

"Some might say they don't believe in heaven. Go and tell it to the man who lives in hell."

"How did you get in here? You are not a student… or are you?"

"No I'm not. But you can imagine how determined I am. I'm not from Manchester nor even England and yet here I am with you AGAIN. Where else on Planet Earth would I be? Where else on Planet Earth would I want to be? No where else is the answer."

"Well your soul is a Manc. That's for sure. I've never met anyone else more Manc. Except you lack the accent."

"I love that you say you have never met anyone else more Manc when you haven't even met me in this life life."

Jen can feel her heart fast drifting into connection with Olivia. She says

"There's a Uni cafe a minute around the corner. Lets go and talk there."

That is music to Olivia's ears.

In the cafe Jen simply blurts out the reason, that Jen had guessed was the reason, for her avoidance. Having heard Olivia accuse her of paranoia she defends her stance by saying

"But this life counts in its own right."

"I know you Jen. You like some drama in life. You are a city girl like me. You couldn't for example live a Castaway life to avoid me could you?"

"Don't have to go that far. And don't want to go that far. I am only here at Uni because I want some social interaction… but I am avoiding *too much* connection to people. I remember Sarah Aston and Lara Hine from previous lives. I'm avoiding them too."

"That should be quite easy given they live in Brooklyn" replies Olivia.

"Not really. Not with social media. I have been primarily avoiding you. But them as well."

"Are you sure this is healthy?" asks a craving Olivia… craving for Jen's love physically and mentally.

"Beats suicide at a concert. Beats being murdered in one's own home. Beats jumping off or being pushed off cliffs. Beats plane crashes" replies Jen. But Olivia would take all of that risk in return for Jen's touch. She wants to watch Jen sleeping at night, feeling her lovers breath on her face. And she wants to kiss her lips and see her undressed. She wants intimacy. She wants to relax over a glass… or many glasses… of wine with her.

But…

… Olivia understands the seriousness of what Jen is saying. And she can see that although she and Jen know that consciousness continues, it is still traumatic stuff, especially for others who do not know anything really about the nature of reality. Maybe, thinks Olivia to herself, Jen is thinking about those others such as parents who suffer so much in this life when something tragic or fatal happens to their daughter. She can empathise with this but she cannot empathise with Jen's plan to avoid her for a whole lifetime.

"I know Jen…" says Olivia planning on a big compromise. She goes quiet for a moment because Olivia considers her own idea that has come to mind a very expensive sacrifice. But she thinks she has no choice but to compromise in favour of something she really dislikes the sound of… because the alternative to compromise is no connection to Jen whatsoever.

"What?" asks Jen.

"Well we know there are an infinite number of lifetimes ahead of us. And what I am going to suggest is a huge compromise on what I ideally want but it will also give you a mission, a purpose… as it will for me. My plan is we do not get together."

As Olivia says that the pain of saying it results in a tear falling from her eye.

"But instead we nurture someone to reach their potential. So I will be able to invest my love I want to give you, and put some of that into nurturing this currently hypothetical person. I think you will have to do this as well, because you need to re-direct the emotion you have for me into something else."

Olivia likes the idea of nurturing someone to reach their potential but to pretend that it can be a substitute for being fully with Jen is simply a lie.

Jen, feeling like crying her eyes out and fearing that if she stays here a second longer she will declare her never ending love for Olivia stands up and says in an assertive tone of voice…

"I will give you 10 days to come up with a plan. Try and impress me."

She scribbles her email address on a piece of A4 paper and hands it to Olivia. She then walks off, tears of love flowing from her eyes that she held back just long enough for Olivia to fail to see those tears…and leaving Olivia no option but to trust that the email address is real. It is real. But that doesn't mean Jen trusts Olivia one single bit. She is convinced that Olivia couldn't possibly stick to a promise to just be friends. She is in-love with her and Jen is every single bit as convinced of that fact as she is convinced about gravity. This means that Jen starts to hatch a plan herself. She is certain that she needs to do this because just telling Olivia to keep her hands off her will just be a constant delay before the two finally crack and end up in the same situation as all the previous lives.

Jen's plan is to test out the rumours that her genius Psychology tutor and lecturer, Professor Stephen Gallagher, cannot resist attractive and smart female students. Jen is after his money so she can move away and this time do a better job of hiding her whereabouts from Olivia. Jen is in a huge rush to do this. She needs money fast and she needs to deflect her longing for Olivia by coming onto another person, man or woman. But there's only Gallagher that she thinks she can come onto fast with success. Well she could come onto a young male student but that is not Jen's style at all… not even in a desperate situation like this one. It may seem arrogant to think she can pull it off in relation to Gallagher, but in Jen's mind this is one of the most important things she will ever do. She lingers outside his office, and then when she sees him approach she smiles at him. He enters his office saying

"Were you waiting for me?"

"Nope."

Jen then stands outside of his office, planning what to do in her head as Gallagher marks essays. It is almost 3 hours later when he exits and Jen has been there all that time. Its now evening and dark outside. She has kept out of sight when he exited his office. But as he enters the dark, rainy and slightly windy Manchester night she follows him and then, from a distance she shouts

"PROFFESSOR GALLAGHER!"

Stephen turns around.

She approaches him with confidence and states

"Its so lonely for me sitting among those kids all the time."

She pauses and stares into his eyes. Jen slightly goes on tip toes and then says to an intrigued Gallagher…

"… I want some intimacy with a man. An intelligent man. Are you intelligent Stephen? Are you a man Stephen?" Jen's eye lashes are practically touching Gallaghers eye brows, and he can feel Jen's breath on his lips.

The Professor cannot believe his luck. He deliberately drops his briefcase to the floor and the two kiss. Jennifer Wilson's plan is working already.

Two days later

Olivia again gets herself into the University and turns up again at one of Jen's Psychology lectures. Jen can't be seen anywhere. Olivia is hoping she is running late.

At the very start of the lecture Gallagher has an announcement to make.

"One of our student's has won £10,000. She entered a competition where a student had to devise a new concept or idea within the world of mental health. This is an international competition with thousands of entrants. Stand up Elizabeth Manton. Take the applause."

The applause goes on for a couple of minutes. Some of the cheering students are planning on making Elizabeth pay for the drinks when they are next out. Gallagher doesn't embarrass her by making her say anything. He speaks for her…

"Elizabeth revised Carl Jung's 'Archetypal' concept. She says that her definition means that the individual must believe their experience is really happening. She focuses on terror. If someone is writing about the terror of seeing a ghost in a fictional piece of work then that individual is not experiencing terror because they don't believe the experience of terror is really happening to themselves. But if he or she is experiencing a nightmare it is terror as they have fallen for it. Its like a temporary brainwashing. Elizabeth inextricably links the Archetypal with Paranoia.

Its paranoid because the terror in nightmares is unnecessary because the individual is safe, simply sleeping. Ditto the same is true in DMT bad trip experiences and in frightening Near Death Experiences. Unlike Jung, Elizabeth doesn't focus on positive psych experiences. More like Freud she thinks we should only be interested in experiences that require the doctor. But like Jung she focuses on these experiences as collective and universal hence archetypal. Jung referred to the Archetypes and the Collective Unconscious. Elizabeth is a little more Freudian sounding with 'The Archetypal and Collective Paranoia.' She's not implying that the individual experiencing a night terror is clinically paranoid. She goes by the DSM on that which requires months of paranoid experience before labelling someone as clinically paranoid. A nightmare, a bad trip or a frightening NDE is temporary. Nevertheless Elizabeth writes *"Such archetypal experiences prove the potential for clinical paranoia in all of us."* She also includes a dictionary definition of her Archetypal concept. She writes

"The Archetypal is inextricably linked to paranoia whereby the terror experienced in nightmares, DMT and terrifying NDE's is genuinely believed to be literally happening. Wrongly. This is universal collective human experience common to all, hence is archetypal."

Gallagher concludes that Elizabeth Manton had to win the admiration of various Psychology organisations such as The International Association of Jungian Studies and The British Psychoanalytical Society.

Olivia then hears a student sat near to her telling another student that there are rumours that Gallagher is sleeping with not only Elizabeth Manton, but also Jen Wilson… and others who the student names.

That same night Olivia email messages Jen:

"Hey Jen, I think I have found the person we should nurture. Her name is Elizabeth Manton. She's a student of Gallagher's. She won 10 grand for an essay she penned that sounds like she unites Freud and Jung in some way. Clearly she has great potential to go far.

I also overheard a student talking some nonsense about how Gallagher is sleeping with you."

Jen messaged back 4 hours later writing

"I am seeing Stephen. I will think about the Manton idea."

Olivia did not feel confident about telling Jen that she heard that Gallagher was sleeping with Manton and others. It would come across as jealousy and an attempt to end Jen's relationship with the Professor. She is so desperate to avoid an extremely painful argument with Jen that she is deliberately being ultra cautious. She doesn't ever want to hear or read Jen saying something to her along the lines of *You don't own me.* It's not that Olivia thinks she does own Jen. Its quite simply that they belong together.

But with evidence it maybe is not a bad idea to let Jen know that Gallagher is sleeping with other women. So Olivia decided to stalk Elizabeth Manton at the end of Psych lectures.

Other students were becoming familiar with seeing Olivia at lectures (although Olivia couldn't attend seminars as she would be found out as an imposter in those classes). Nevertheless she is now considered a mature Psychology student by most who attend Gallaghers lectures. Wrongly considered a mature student of course.

Olivia paid a male student £125 the other day just for his swipe card. He never turned up to get it back at the arranged destination but Olivia plans to hand it in to the receptionist at some point.

Jen, despite now seeing Gallagher, is again a no-show at his lecture. Olivia is convinced that she is avoiding her. At the end of the lecture, Olivia follows Elizabeth out of the lecture hall, and out of the building. Manton heads for the car park and stands next to someone's car. Clearly not her own car as she just stopped there waiting around for someone. Then in the distance Olivia spots Gallagher walking towards the car park. Olivia hasn't driven here so she see's some young looking male student heading towards their car. Olivia calls to him and says

"Hey, I will pay you £150 cash in hand if you follow this car wherever it goes." Olivia does not care that she is paying so much money out as she thinks it is all worth it.

"DEAL!!!" shouts the cash strapped student excitedly.

Gallagher and Manton get in the Professors car. 20 minutes later its parking up outside the Gallaghers impressive looking large house.

11 Weeks Earlier

Elizabeth Manton enters Professor Stephen Gallagher's office.

"What can I do for you Elizabeth?" asks the Psychology lecturer and tutor while he admires the beauty of his young 20 year old student.

Elizabeth has come here to get with the Professor. But she has no intention of just blurting that out. She says instead

"Well in this essay you have set for us we have to discuss Jung and/or Freud in the 21st century. But I think all of their original work is just fine. So I am wondering if you can help with that?"

The student is slightly embarrassed about asking that question. She is perfectly well aware of what she is supposed to do. She is well versed in Post Jungian and Post Freudian thinkers. But she has planned what she's saying here and later intends to admit to Gallagher that this question was just her way of getting into his pants. Gallagher looks into Elizabeth's beautiful eyes and responds

"Choose Freud or Jung. Outline a key concept or two of theirs. Then bring in someone… for example Lacan if its Freud… or for example, Giegerich if its Jung… and outline their revision of the originals work and then side with the original. Undermine the Post Jungian or Post Freudian thinkers ideas and embrace the original. And explain your reasoning. Say why you support the original thinker and say why you reject the later thinker. But you are my smartest student by miles. So you already know that. So why are you really here Elizabeth?"

Elizabeth leans forward. Gallagher looks relaxed, in his natural environment, books and essays sprawled out all over his desk. It looks messy but its an organised mess. Elizabeth swipes all of that organised mess onto the floor, leans forwards and grabs Gallagher by his shirt. She is now on all fours on the Professors desk. This is Gallaghers dream come true. She is right to have believed the rumours about him and right to have confidence in herself. A surprised Gallagher shouts

"WAIT". He gets up and locks the door. He then has sex in his office with his young student. He never once considered the risks. Now if Elizabeth demands an A Grade in an essay he can hardly say no lest she tells the educational authorities about what he and she have done together. But in Elizabeth Manton's mind, this coming onto her professor, is about a lot more than just getting A Grades. For starters she wants Gallagher to write an entire essay on a new conceptual idea so she can enter it into a competition with her name on the front cover. A competition with a £10,000 prize. Elizabeth Manton now has power over the Professor and she intends to use it.

Location: Manchester, England. Prof Stephen Gallagher's House.

Present Day

Olivia who has waited patiently for a couple of hours outside of Gallaghers house. She watches as his front door opens. Out steps Elizabeth. Then outsteps Gallagher. They kiss just outside the door. Olivia takes as many photo's as she can. Just as Elizabeth leaves, Jen arrives. The timing is so close that Olivia interprets it as a near disaster for Gallagher.

Location: Stockport, England. Olivia's House.

Late that night, Olivia emails Jen. Things are complicated for Olivia now. She wants Jen to end whatever it is she has with Gallagher. And she wants to nurture Elizabeth with Jen. But sending those pics, Olivia thinks, will achieve the former goal but vanquish the latter goal. And she needs the nurturing idea in order to maintain a connection with Jen. So she simply asks

"Do you believe the rumours about Gallagher seeing multiple women at the same time? Or is that all a load of nonsense?"

Jen replies to the email with

"Its true about Stephen. I originally wanted him in order to make a lot of money and then move elsewhere. I admit I wanted to escape from you… not because I don't love you, but because I do love you. But Stephen could see right through me. He likes that I need fixing. He likes that I have trust issues. He says our relationship has no expectations, no conditions. Nothing is expected of me, and I should not expect anything of him. We are free to see other people, we are free to sleep with other people. I like the feeling of being so free."

Olivia instantly realises that the timing of Elizabeth leaving and Jen arriving was no near disaster for anyone although she has raised eyebrows over the Professors lack of professionalism. She responds to Jen with another email saying

"Ok, I respect 100% that is your private business with Stephen. None of my business. But is Elizabeth Manton and her development our potential business? I would like it to be so."

"Hey Olivia. Good news. The answer is YES! We have a deal!!!!! Let's make Elizabeth Manton the next Freud or Jung. I will contact Sarah Aston… It would be great for Elizabeth to chat with a psychiatrist who might be able to help advance her career."

Two days later

Its not long before Jen and Olivia persuade Elizabeth to chat through video link online with Sarah Aston. Elizabeth likes the idea of a top New York City psychiatrist being part of her networking.

Sarah) So are you coming from a Freudian psychoanalytical starting point or from a Jungian psych starting point?

Elizabeth) Psychoanalysis.

Sarah) Let me see if I have got this right. You start from a psychoanalytical perspective. You then take the Jungian archetypal concept but not the archetype. Because its the experience of the archetypal that you solely focus on. But in true Freudian style the concept becomes medical. You are not interested in the spiritual or positive psychological experiences because they are not a medical problem. So you focus on the experience of unnecessary archetypal terror. And because its unnecessary you link it to paranoia. Paranoia is a very medical concept in its own right. But because of the example experiences (nightmares, bad trip DMT, negative experiences in the NDE such as the Void) being temporary, the archetypal terror is not clinically diagnosed as paranoia. This is because the DSM diagnosis requires months of ongoing symptoms before diagnosing someone as clinically paranoid. However you do say that their universal experience of unnecessary terror is, as said, universal, thus common to the point of all humans experiencing it. Thus you conclude unnecessary terror is a profoundly archetypal experience that proves the potential paranoia existing in ALL of us. There's countless individual social relationship paranoia cases. But the unconscious nightmare, DMT, NDE terror cases demonstrate the paranoia in all of us. Its the latter, in all of us, archetypal paranoia cases you are interested in."

Elizabeth) "Thank you. I couldn't have worded it better myself."

Sarah) Well you did. In that essay. That's why you are 10 grand better off. My question to you Elizabeth, is, why do you think this is such a good improvement on Jung?

Elizabeth) I want the Psych field to focus on… why do humans all experience paranoia? We need to see through it in order to individually and collectively cure. I want the Psych field to focus on that. With Jung's concept I think the Psych field lacked focus as his archetypes concept is all over the place. Stick to the medical.

Sarah) You are so good for a 20 year old. I'm interested in psych ideas you think are really good that are not discussed in your essay. Can you touch on one or two of those?

Elizabeth) The individual needs to kill their favourite icon.

Sarah) Like the Buddhist saying "If you see the Buddha, kill the Buddha".

Elizabeth) Yes. Exactly. You haven't grown up until you have killed your hero.

Sarah) Or kill multiple figures. Most people have more than one hero… more than one ego identification.

Elizabeth) Yup. Kill your hero then the other hero then the other hero and so on and so on. You need to kill your ego for mental health. Your ego is an army. Its not just 1 person nor just one thing.

Sarah) And its a projection. It pretends (including pretending to itself) that its about these other figures… or the army as you say. But they are just used for itself. The ego is in love with itself.

Elizabeth) Narcissism.

Sarah) Indeed. Its a fake outward looking.

Elizabeth) Its identification with oneself. But its projected out. It is always projected out. You see through yourself by seeing through the multiple identifications. Achieving that equates to killing one's ego.

Sarah) So while many students look to left wing politics you look to…?

Elizabeth) An outer world attack on fascism is one thing. Lesbians and gays achieved that when the masses managed to see through the now obvious to see prejudices. But the greatest attack on fascism for the individual would be to see through their own narcissistic individual ego.

Sarah) That's a profound point you make Elizabeth. What is your answer to those who may argue you strip life of its colour?

Elizabeth) The keyword here is impermanence. You don't cling to what has gone. You enjoy, even identify in the moment. That is healthy. But then you let go. You can identify with something else in the next moment. But always let go. Otherwise what you call colour becomes anxiety. Again, recognizing the impermanence of all things is so important.

Sarah) I am going to get you some publicity in the New York press.

Elizabeth) The New York Times???

Sarah) Don't know yet. We'll see. But whatever the publication, it will lead to more coverage as it snowballs once you have made your name in this city. Don't let it go to your head though. That would be extra hypocritical considering your outlook.

Elizabeth) inlook.

Jen and Olivia were sat watching this discussion. They considered it excellent early progress concerning their nurturing.

Once Sarah has said goodbye… the young student says to Jen and Olivia that there is something she just needs to tell someone.

"What is it you want to tell us?"

Elizabeth sighs and hesitates but still manages to blurt it out…

"I have just had to tell someone this… I just can't keep it to myself. I don't know what the urge to tell someone is, despite my apparent genius" Elizabeth said that while simultaneously laughing. She continues

"You know I am really, genuinely smart when it comes to Psychology, discussing it and so on."

"Yes. Clearly." replies Jen.

Elizabeth scews her face and says

"But maybe not as smart in this field as I am making myself out to be."

Olivia and Jen are surprised by the statement. Their natural instinct is to disagree.

"What the hell makes you say that?" asks Jen.

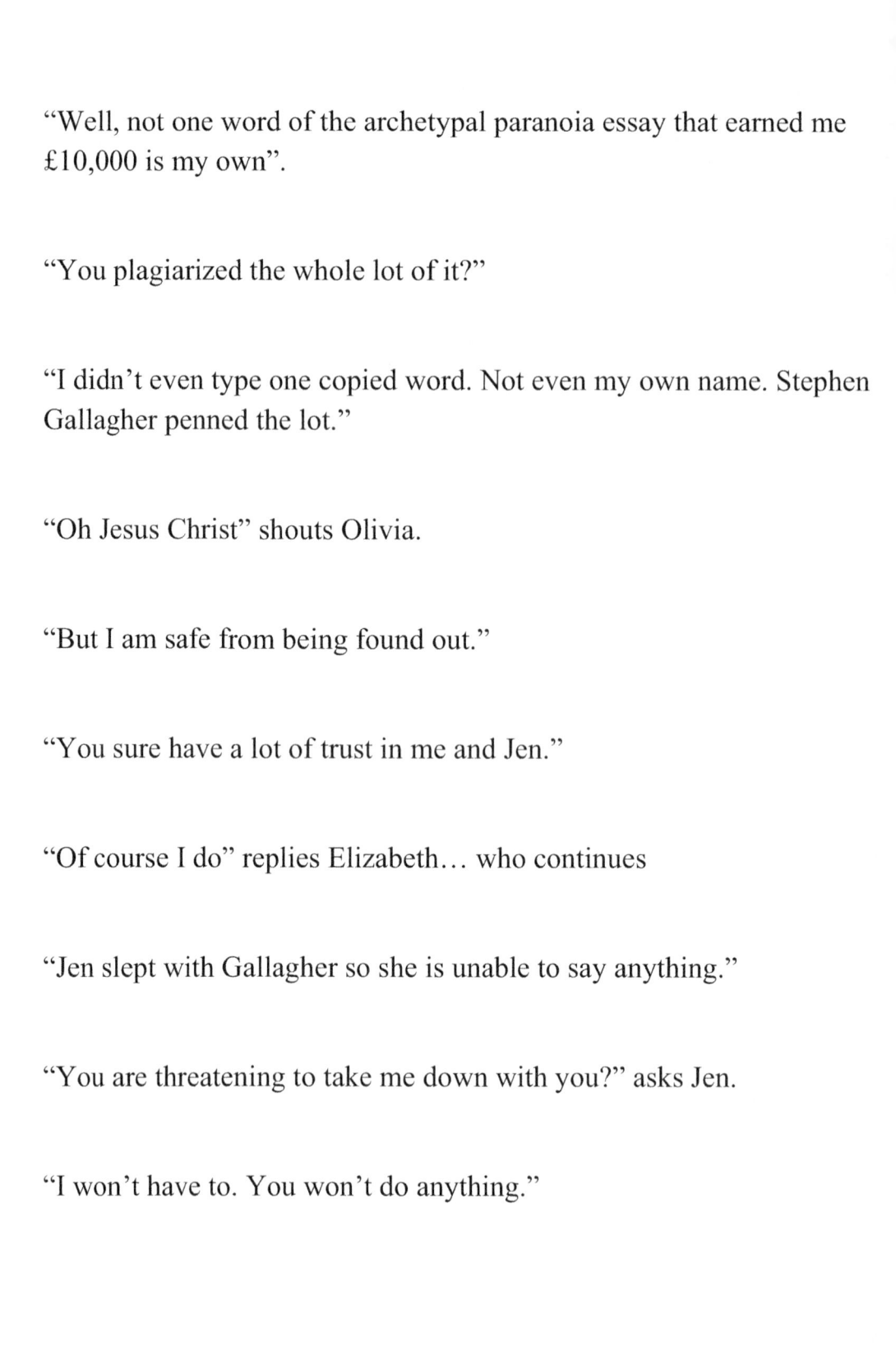

"Well, not one word of the archetypal paranoia essay that earned me £10,000 is my own".

"You plagiarized the whole lot of it?"

"I didn't even type one copied word. Not even my own name. Stephen Gallagher penned the lot."

"Oh Jesus Christ" shouts Olivia.

"But I am safe from being found out."

"You sure have a lot of trust in me and Jen."

"Of course I do" replies Elizabeth… who continues

"Jen slept with Gallagher so she is unable to say anything."

"You are threatening to take me down with you?" asks Jen.

"I won't have to. You won't do anything."

That is of course a possibility. Elizabeth may be right. Why would a 32 year old mature student want the grief of publicity of sleeping with their psychology lecturer? But of course Jen and Olivia are good friends with Sarah Aston and they are not fake friends. And Sarah is helping them simply because they requested it. Hence Elizabeth has underestimated Jen's loyalty to Sarah Aston, even if she has been avoiding her. Remember she avoids these people because she cares about them.

"So you blackmailed Gallagher?" asks Jen.

"When I first entered his office, I already knew my plan. I went with a question about my essay, knowing fine well that I would come onto him and then blackmail him to write my essay entry for the 10 grand prize. I want him to write a book with my name on the front of it next time. But I do understand everything he says. And even better, he still likes me despite the power dynamics being in my favour. He is quite liberated when you think about it."

Olivia has her head in her hands. She with an anguished and slightly angry tone responds

"Can you not see how this contradicts your message. This is a narcissistic power ego psychology on your part. That will be all the more humiliating for you when you get found out."

Jen adds "Stephen's career will be over and rightly so. I will not see him anymore that is for certain."

Olivia is relieved about what Jen just said but is simultaneously feeling angrier each passing minute in relation to Elizabeth. She hits out at the young student.

"You are such an idiot Elizabeth. You are bright. If you had to do some scheming you should have merely used it to get more mentoring out of Gallagher. Instead this entire thing is one gigantic unethical, unprofessional, wreaking of academic corruption mess. That 10 thousand pounds doesn't belong to you."

"So who does it belong to?"

"Whoever came second" replies Jen.

"I'm not all bad. I just want the money and then I actually intend to work on that psychology. There's something to it. I really can see it sounds right. But I want comfort as my base from which to work."

Olivia makes direct eye contact with Elizabeth and in an ordering tone of voice says…

"Go home Elizabeth. I want to talk to Jen about this."

Elizabeth, still quite pleased with what she has done, thinking she has won, gets up and leaves.

Within three minutes of leaving Olivia and Jen agree to contact Sarah Aston and tell her to not do Elizabeth any favours as the essay is all her tutor and lecturers work. News soon spreads of Elizabeths and Stephen Gallaghers unprofessionalism. Gallagher doesn't wait to be fired from Manchester Uni. He quits.

News spreads fast about Gallagher and Manton.

3 days later

Sarah Aston had tried hard to get Jen and Olivia to find and comfort Elizabeth. But they could not find her anywhere. She had gone missing. But she did turn up… dead. Elizabeth Manton is tragically found dead on the University premises, following taking a massive overdose of paracetamol swished down with a massive intake of vodka.

At first Jen blames herself and Olivia. She even utters the words *"You don't own me"* to Olivia. But within weeks she accepts that the young students suicide is a tragic coincidence and that she and Olivia are innocent and had only good intentions with regards to Elizabeth.

1 Year Anniversary of Elizabeth Manton's Suicide: Jennifer Wilson's house: Night time

Jen and Olivia down a lot of wine. They make love. They end the night singing and dancing to Oasis', *Some Might Say*.

Soundtrack

Can I in true Elizabeth Manton style just use someone else's soundtrack and pass it off as my own? Ha. i.e., the soundtrack from the Queens Gambit please. Main Title — YouTube

Additional Notes

- For those who worry that Jen and Olivia should not be in partying mood on the anniversary of a 20 year old's suicide, our loveable Mancs (yeah I know Olivia is from Brooklyn but she's definitely a Manc!) are 100% aware that Elizabeth's consciousness continues. Elizabeth believed in Gallaghers psychology in the end. It was just too late to prove it. Tragically, easily enough to cry your heart out, she died considered a hypocrite and a cheat BUT in the world I have created here, everyone has a soul. At 20 years old she hadn't quite matured but her brain was on fire… she needed a little more time. Jen and Olivia KNOW that Elizabeth has literally an infinite number of chances. So they have no guilt singing, dancing and getting drunk exactly 1 year after Elizabeth's suicide.

- In the story Olivia answered a question about whether or not she is a Man Utd fan by answering "Stockers actually" (i.e. Stockport County). But is that the truth? The truth is she is totally in-love with all things Manchester… United, City and because of Jen being from Stockport, also Stockport County. She even loves the Trafford Centre. And its all as if its in honour of Jen! ... I wouldn't say she's a Stockport fan but she would certainly wear a Stockport County scarf without hesitation. But more than anything she would wear an 'OASIS OLIVIA' T-Shirt... or maybe both the Stockport scarf and Oasis Olivia T Shirt at the same time. But with Oasis connection to Manchester City FC... she would also wear a Man City scarf or top. So there's a preference to City and County over Man Utd. In past lives she has bantered Jen over her Manc status but this has evolved into her becoming a Manc herself. Rather than mocking Stockport (for their smallness) she has started to talk them up... pointing out that she would like one night to do what she wants with that cool, seriously hot Stockport Manc, Michelle Keegan. To which Jen responded with half joking jealously growl... "Ggggrrrr".

- In one of Jen and Olivia's infinite number of lives, Olivia met Jen and the first thing she did was to sing the following Oasis lyrics into her ear... well she sang those lyrics in a whispering singing style into Jen's ear. Jen instantly recognised the song as if the song were her own. But Oasis had never released a song called *Roll with it*... that is — not in the timeline that Olivia sang it into Jen's ear.

- Olivia went from playful teasing of Jen being Stockport born and bred... to loving all things Manchester and thus being unable to even mock anymore as there is no one more Manc than her... at the end of Part 1 of Book 6 (the book called Sectioned). Its this paragraph where the change has 100% occurred. *Olivia Hargreaves is at the Oasis concert. She has stood seemingly in a trance wearing a Stockport County scarf as the other fans sing and shout the lyrics of each song played, and cheer at the start and end of each song. Tears keep flowing down Oliva's face. Eventually Oasis start singing the song she has been waiting for. They start singing Live Forever. More tears flow down Olivia's face. Her mental agony is a level of torture she wouldn't wish on anyone. She stuffs her mouth full of something before swilling whatever she has consumed down with a bottle of water. She collapses. Those fans closest to her think she is drunk. But within seconds she's dead, having deliberately taken a massive overdose of Jen's prescribed Somnexil medication that Jen never took.*

Paranoia is Book 7 in the series.

Book 1

Abduction inspired UFO Disclosure is only the Start

Reading time: 111 minutes

Book 2

The Void

Reading time: 65 minutes

Book 3

Who were We?

Reading time: 56 minutes

Book 4

Freedom

Reading time: 55 minutes

Book 5

The Sign

Reading time: 60 minutes

Book 6

SECTIONED

Reading time: 51 minutes

Book 7

Paranoia

Reading time: 30 minutes

Printed in Great Britain
by Amazon